D0883913

The
FORGIVENESS
GARDEN

by LAUREN THOMPSON
pictures by CHRISTY HALE

FEIWEL AND FRIENDS
NEW YORK

A NOTE *on the* NAMES

The names in this story are drawn from the Sanskrit language, an ancient language in which many of the sacred writings of Hinduism, Buddhism, and other religions were written. It is also related to many languages of Southeast Asia, Western Asia, and Europe.

Vayam – [vah-yahm] "Us"
Gamte – [gahm-tay] based on *Graama Tayoh*, "Village of Them"
Sama – [sah-mah] based on *Ksama*, "Forgiveness"
Karune – [kah-roon] based on *Karunya*, "Kindness"

A FEIWEL AND FRIENDS BOOK
An Imprint of Macmillan

THE FORGIVENESS GARDEN. Text copyright © 2012 by Lauren Thompson.
Illustrations copyright © 2012 by Christy Hale. All rights reserved. Printed in China
by RR Donnelley Asia Printing Solutions Ltd., Dongguan City, Guangdong Province. For information, address
Feiwel and Friends, 175 Fifth Avenue, New York, N.Y. 10010.

Library of Congress Cataloging-in-Publication Data Available

ISBN: 978-0-312-62599-3

The collage artwork was created with mixed media.

Book design by Christy Hale

Feiwel and Friends logo designed by Filomena Tuosto

First Edition: 2012

10 9 8 7 6 5 4 3 2

mackids.com

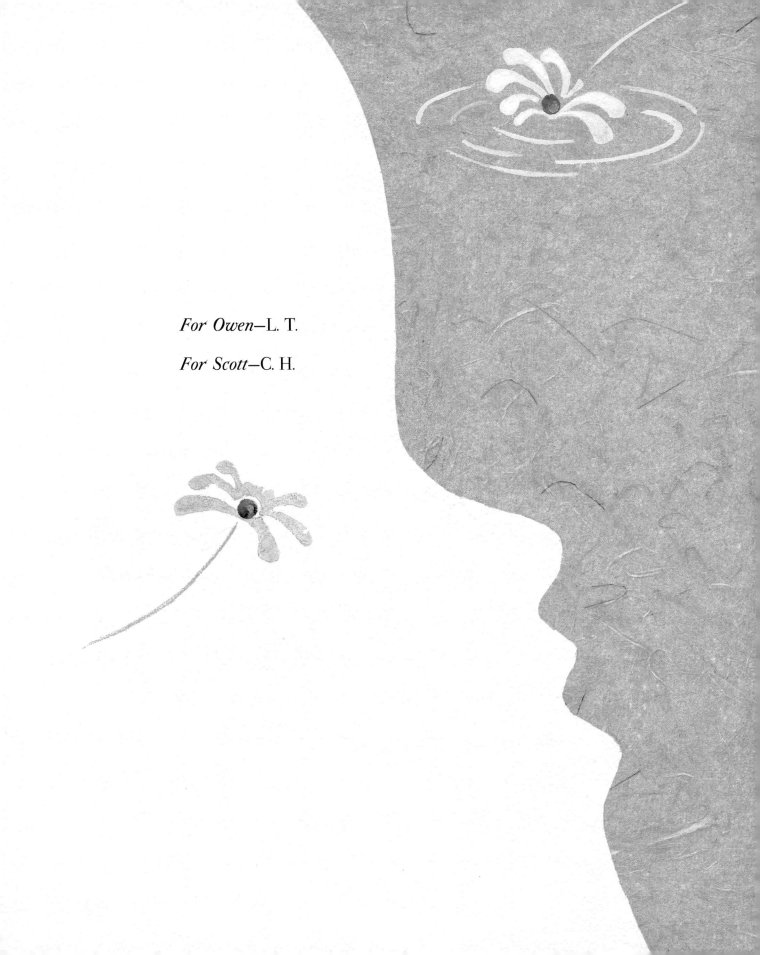

For Owen—L. T.

For Scott—C. H.

There was a valley, and through the valley ran a stream. The village of Vayam stood on one side, and the village of Gamte stood on the other.

There was no peace in the valley. For the two villages had hated each other for a long, long time.

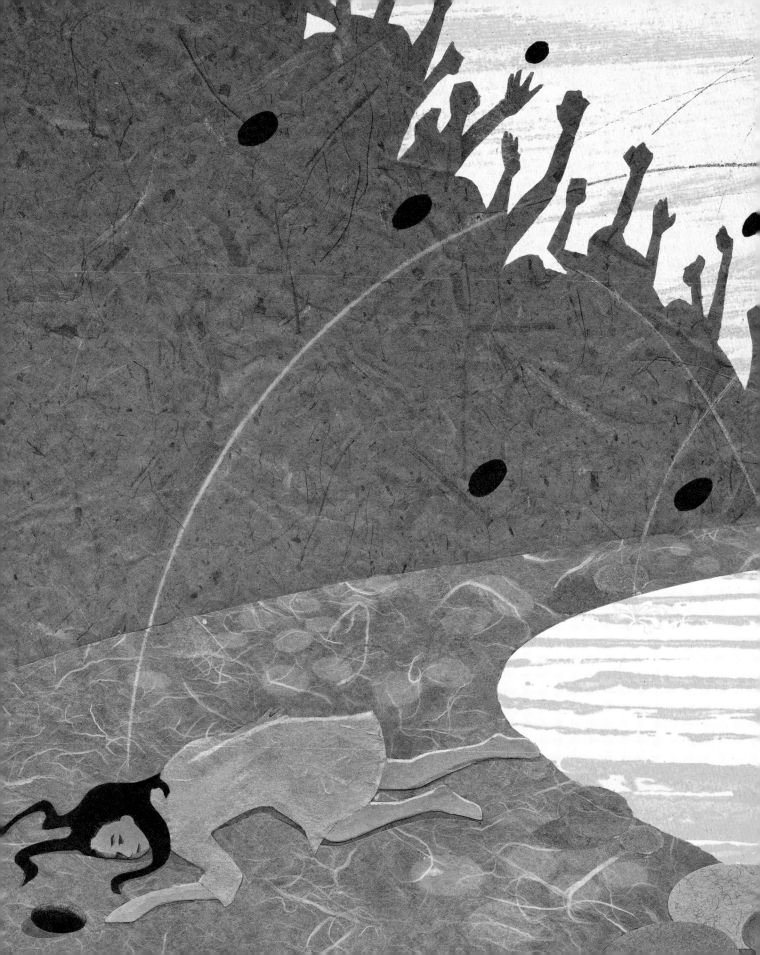

One day, a new argument sparked. Both villages claimed a certain part of the stream as their own. Angry words flew across the stream. Then stones.

A Gamte boy, named Karune, picked up a large stone and hurled it across the water.

A Vayam girl, named Sama, stood where the stone fell. The stone hit Sama hard on the head, and she fell hard to the ground.

The villagers of Vayam ran to help. The villagers of Gamte cheered and ran away. The Vayams called out for revenge. They were angry. And they were afraid. *Would the Gamtes never stop fighting us?*

They gathered around Sama, admiring her courage and plotting their revenge against the Gamtes. As days passed, Sama's pain began to lessen, but her hatred of the Gamtes grew.

And in the village of Gamte, too, the people were angry.
And they were afraid. *Would the Vayams fight us always?*

They gathered around Karune, praising his courage
and scheming how to defend against the Vayams.
Karune secretly wondered how brave he had
truly been. But his hatred for the Vayams only grew.

One day, Sama walked along the stream, yearning for something to ease her aching, angry heart. She reached a calm pool and bent to drink. What she saw reflected there stopped her. She saw the ugly scar, but most of all, she saw her own dark, brooding scowl.

"Who have I become?" she cried.

Sama wept for a long time.

Then Sama looked across the stream. There, a few children from Gamte walked together. How scared and angry and sad they looked! Sama's heart softened.

"They are just like us," she thought.

Suddenly, a few of Sama's own people ran up. "Here you are!" they shouted. "The time for revenge has come!" And they pulled her away to join the fight.

Villagers from Vayam and Gamte crowded the stream. The Vayams held a captive: It was Karune. And they all held stones.

A large stone was put into Sama's hands. It was the stone that Karune had thrown.

"Throw the stone at him!" her people hissed. "Throw it hard!"

Sama looked at all the villagers, those from Vayam
and those from Gamte. Their faces were like hers had
been, hardened with anger and fear and hate.

Suddenly, Sama knew what she had to do. "No!" she said in a loud, clear voice. "I won't hurt him! Let the boy go!"

Her people grumbled. Sama went on.

"It's time to stop the fighting," she said. "We must stop hurting and hating." And she flung the large stone to the ground.

"Let us build a garden instead," she said.

Now, all of the people grumbled. Someone shouted, "What kind of garden?"

Sama knew. "A forgiveness garden."

Some people gasped, some scoffed. Some just laughed.

But some from Vayam murmured, "If Sama wants it . . ."

They let Karune go. Then, they piled their stones near Sama's.

Some from Gamte saw this and murmured, "It's worth a try. . . ."
They added stones of their own.

Only Karune hung back, scared, angry.

Stone by stone, the people of the valley built a garden wall together. But they had questions.

"If we forgive, must we forget all that has happened?" asked the villagers of Vayam.

Sama answered, "We will sit together in the garden and decide."

"Must we apologize?" asked the villagers of Gamte. "Will the Vayams apologize?"

Sama answered, "The garden will help us find what is right."

Still, Karune stayed apart, watching and thinking.

Villagers set flowers into the soil and planted a tree. When the garden was complete, its loveliness made everyone smile.

"This garden is for all of us," Sama said. "It can help us to put aside hate and learn what forgiveness feels like. Who will join me?"

At first, no one moved. No one dared. The two villages had
hated each other for a long, long time. It was hard to try a new way.
Then Karune, brave Karune, stepped forward.
"I will join you," he said to Sama.

Sama, of Vayam, and Karune, of Gamte, stepped
into the garden together. They sat under the tree.
And they began to talk.

What do you think they said?

About the
GARDENS *of* FORGIVENESS
FOUNDATION
by
Reverend Lyndon Harris

The Garden of Forgiveness is in Beirut, Lebanon, and is the vision of Alexandra Asseily, humanitarian, activist, and psychotherapist, who has declared that "every act of revenge is a time bomb thrown into the future." It was created in the aftermath of a civil war that claimed 300,000 lives (1985–2000).

In 2005, I was privileged to take family members who lost loved ones in the tragic events of 9/11 in New York City to plant an olive tree for peace in the Garden of Forgiveness. Standing there on that hallowed ground, we pledged to bring Alexandra's vision to New York and to the world. As Archbishop Desmond Tutu said, "There is no future without forgiveness."

ABOUT LYNDON HARRIS

The Reverend Lyndon Harris was the priest in charge of Saint Paul's Chapel, the church directly across the street from the World Trade Center that he helped convert into a rescue operation, serving the needs of the men and women who courageously faced the challenges of rescuing survivors and ultimately recovering the remains of the dead. Saint Paul's Chapel served over half a million meals to rescue workers and was open around the clock for eight and a half months. Harris is now the Executive Director of the Gardens of Forgiveness, a U.S.–based educational nonprofit committed to teaching forgiveness. For more information and to download a Garden of Forgiveness start-up kit, please go to www.forgivetogive.org.